For Lena.
Again and always.

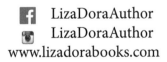
LizaDoraAuthor
LizaDoraAuthor
www.lizadorabooks.com

Edited by Jolie Gray

ISBN: 978-0-692-88259-7

BE
STILL

a bedtime book of faith

by Liza Dora

BE
NOT
AFRAID

of mountains tall...

...or waters that run
too deep.

For you, My darling love...

...are always in MY

KEEP.

Be brave in the face of

GIANTS...

...be kind to those both little and small...

...because, My precious one...

...I have

DOMINION

over all.

Push against the night,

but always be welcome of the...

STARS.

The light they shine upon you...

...I've planned from afar.

Look
for Me
in flowers...

...and in the
faces
of
your
friends.

I'm found in the humblest of places...

...yet, My

KINGDOM

has no end.

My love knows no bounds.

It has no edges and no seams.

My

GRACE is sufficient...

...for all those who believe.

BE STILL,

My love, and know...

...as you drift off to dream...

I AM.

I WAS.

I'M

ALWAYS...

...and through
My Son you are redeemed.

Available From Liza Dora Books

Now Available in Middle Grade...

Shop all titles at lizadorabooks.com

CPSIA information can be obtained
at www.ICGtesting.com
Printed in the USA
LVHW070057271020
669841LV00046B/148